Are You Listening, Jack?

by Ellen Garcia • illustrated by Julia Patton

"Why don't you have your coat on, Jack?"
asked Miss Jan. "Did you hear me?"

"I guess not," I said.

"Why aren't you in line, Jack?" Miss Jan called. "Did you hear me?"

4

"I guess not," I said.

"Are you listening, Jack?" asked Miss Jan.

"Can you tell me what the story is about?"

I couldn't.

"You need some quiet time," Miss Jan said.

"I have to sit all alone?" I asked.

"You can return when you are ready to listen."

"Eva is going to tell us about her dinosaur," said Miss Jan. "Are you ready to listen?"

"I am ready," I said.

"This dinosaur had wings," Eva said.

I never knew some dinosaurs had wings.

I raised my hand.

"Yes, Jack?" Miss Jan asked.

"Did that dinosaur have feathers, too?" I asked.

"That's a great question, Jack," Miss Jan said.
"Let's find out together!"